D0894713

Stories From Panchatantra

SHREE

Stories From PANCHATANTRA

ISBN - 81-7963-024-2

Published by

SHREE BOOK CENTRE

98/B, Dalmia Building, T.H. Kataria Marg
Matunga (W), Mumbai - 400 016
Tel: 24377516, 24374559 Telefax: 24309183
Email:shreebk@vsnl.com

© Publishers

All rights reserved. No part of this publication may be reproduced, stored in or introduced into a retrieval system transmitted in any form by any means (Electronic, Mechanical, Photocopying, Recording or otherwise) without prior written permission of the Publishers.

Printed in India

CONTENTS

THE RABBIT AND THE LION

Once upon a time, a cruel lion ruled over the jungle. He often killed other animals for no reason. One day all the animals in the jungle gathered together and decided to find a solution to their problem.

The animals went to the lion and pleaded with him not to hunt and kill them. Instead, they promised to offer him one animal as prey from their midst everyday. The lion agreed to their pleas.

One day it was the turn of the rabbit to go to the lion. His poor wife and son cried piteously. But the rabbit was not afraid. He was a very clever rabbit. He was sure that he would find some way of escaping the lion.

The rabbit took a long time to go to the lion's den. It was well past the lion's meal time and he was waiting angrily. He roared furiously when he saw the tiny rabbit. But the clever little rabbit had his reason ready.

The lion grew even more furious when he heard that there was another lion in his jungle. The clever little rabbit led the lion to an old well and pointed towards it from afar.

The foolish lion rushed to the well and roared mightily. From inside came an answering roar. He peeped in and saw another lion looking up at him. It was his reflection! He jumped in to fight. There was a loud splash, and that was the end of the wicked lion.

Moral: Victory does not always go to the strongest.

THE CLEVER MONKEY AND THE CROCODILE

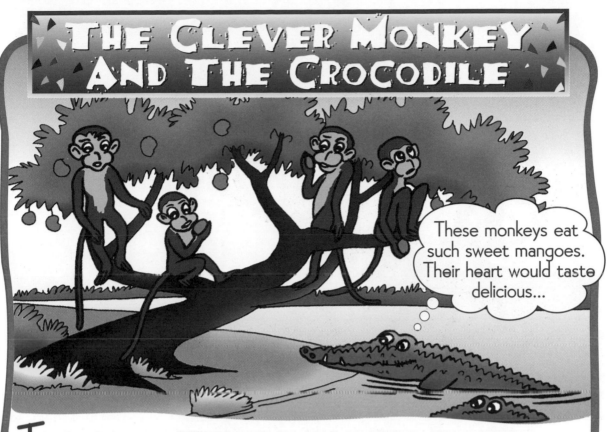

These monkeys eat such sweet mangoes. Their heart would taste delicious...

Two crocodiles once lived in a river. On the banks of that river was a huge mango tree bearing delicious mangoes. A group of monkeys lived on the tree. The crocodiles wanted to catch the monkeys as prey.

One day the crocodiles came up with a plan. They decided to get friendly with the monkeys. It would be then easy to catch them. So one of the crocodiles went up to the monkeys with an invitation.

One of the monkeys agreed to go. He climbed on to the crocodile's back. Soon they were on their way. But when they reached the middle of the river, the monkey was in for a shock!

The monkey realised that he was in grave danger. He thought fast, and soon he had a plan. He started laughing so loudly that the crocodile asked him why he was laughing so much.

The foolish crocodile believed the monkey's story and swam back to the river bank so that the monkey could come back with his heart.

When the other monkeys heard the story, they all laughed and jeered at the foolish crocodile. Thus the clever monkey escaped with his life from the wicked crocodile.

Moral: Presence of mind is the greatest of all abilities.

THE SWANS AND THE TURTLE

A long time ago, two swans and a turtle lived in a pond in the forest. The swans and the turtle were very good friends.

But they were worried. It had not rained the whole year and the water level of the pond was slowly going down.

So the two swans decided to find another larger pond which they and their friend the turtle could make their homes. They flew for a long distance and at last saw another pond. It was bigger, deeper and full of fishes.

The turtle was indeed very happy to hear that the swans had found another pond where they could live. But there was still one problem, the turtle could not fly. Even on land, he could move only very slowly.

But the swans loved their friend the turtle dearly. They thought hard and then one of them had a wonderful plan. He looked around and found a sturdy stick.

The plan was that the swans would hold the stick with their beaks; the turtle would hold the centre of the stick with his mouth. But there was a danger. If any of them spoke on the way, the turtle would fall to his death.

The swans were soon flying high in the air across a small village. The people looked up and were amazed at the sight of two swans carrying a turtle in the sky.

Hearing the people praise the swans for their cleverness, the turtle was filled with envy. He felt that if it wasn't for his courage, they would not have won so much praise. He had to let them know that he had a part too.

The swans were shocked to see their dear friend turtle falling. They desperately tried to clutch at him as he fell but it was useless. In no time he had fallen to his death.

The two swans were filled with sorrow for their foolish friend. Long after they arrived safely at their new home they still missed their good friend the turtle.

Moral: A wise man thinks before he speaks.

The Crows And The Serpent

This is such a wonderful place to build our nest. Soon we will have our babies.

Once upon a time two crows built their nest on a tree next to a pond. The crows loved their little nest. It was close to the palace where the King and Queen lived. Everyday the Queen would come with her maids for a bath in the pond.

Under the same tree lived a huge snake. When Mother Crow laid her eggs, the wicked snake climbed up the tree and swallowed them. The poor crows could not do anything to save their eggs.

The crows were very unhappy. Mother Crow cried all the time thinking of her eggs. Soon they would have more eggs but the wicked snake would come again. Father Crow thought hard. He had to find a way to save their eggs.

Just then the Queen came with her
maids to take a bath in the pond.
Seeing her go by, Father Crow
suddenly had an idea. He quickly told
Mother Crow what he had in mind.

The crows waited for the Queen and her maids to enter the water. Then Father Crow flew around them, cawing loudly to gain their attention. They looked up to see a crow picking up the Queen's precious necklace. It was Mother Crow.

From his perch on the tree Father Crow could see that their plan was working. As Mother Crow picked up the Queen's necklace, the Queen and her maids called out to the palace guards.

Hearing the Queen call, the guard came running with a stick. Mother Crow flew with the necklace and dropped it under the tree next to the snake's hole.

Just when the guard bent down to pick up the jewel, the snake came out to see what all that noise was about. Seeing the snake the guard beat him to death with the stick. Thus the clever crows were able to get rid of the wicked snake.

Moral: Cleverness helps defeat enemies.

THE INDIGO JACKAL

Once upon a time, a jackal hungry for many days, wandered into a village that lay at the edge of the forest. He knew that the village was a dangerous place for him and moved carefully.

Suddenly there was the sound of furious barking. The jackal turned around to see a whole pack of dogs charging at him. The poor jackal ran for his life.

The poor jackal desperately looked for a place to hide. Suddenly he saw a large vat behind a hut. He jumped into the vat. It was full of a foul-smelling liquid.

When the jackal jumped out of the foul-smelling vat, he saw the dogs waiting for him. But to his surprise, the moment they saw him, they yelped with fear and ran away.

The poor jackal went to a pond to quench his thirst. As he bent down to drink, he jumped up in fear. A strange, blue creature looked up at him. But he soon realised that it was only his reflection. He had an idea...

When the jackal went to the forest, all the animals of the forest too were afraid of him. He called them together and told them that he was sent down from heaven to rule over them. They all believed him.

All the animals of the forest willingly served the jackal. One night the jackal suddenly woke up. There was a full moon and the jackals were howling at the moon. He threw back his head and howled too.

The other animals were shocked to hear their heavenly king howl like a common jackal. They realised that they had been tricked. They all fell on him and gave him a sound beating.

Moral: Appearance does not change character

THE WISE FROG

Ekkabudhi was a frog who lived in a pond with his wife. There were many fishes in the pond. The frogs and the fishes were good friends.

One evening two fishermen returning home with the day's catch from the river, passed by the pond. They were surprised to see the pond full of fishes.

The fishermen decided to come the next day and cast their nets in the pond. Ekkabudhi who was resting at the pond's edge heard them speak.

Ekkabudhi went to the fishes and warned them of the great danger they were all in.

But the fishes did not pay heed to his warning. They just laughed at his concern, and tried to comfort him.

But Ekkabudhi was a wise frog. He and his wife decided to leave the pond before the fishermen cast their nets.

Soon afterwards, the fishermen came and cast their net several times into the pond. As much as they would try to escape, all the fishes were soon caught in the net.

Ekkabudhi and his wife watched in horror as they saw their poor friends being caught and taken away by the fishermen.

Moral: Prepare for trouble and you will escape it.

THE DONKEY WHO WOULD SING

A donkey once lived in a forest. He had no friends. One day a fox seeing how lonely the donkey was, went up to him and offered to be his friend.

From that day onwards, the donkey and the fox became good friends. They met with each other often and spent a lot of time together.

One moonlit evening the fox and the donkey met together as they usually did. It was a pleasant evening and they sat together enjoying each other's company.

After a while they both felt hungry and decided to go out looking for food. As they wandered, they came to the edge of the jungle. And there before them was a field full of watermelons.

When they had eaten their fill, the fox turned to leave. But the donkey stopped him.

The fox tried to caution the donkey about making a noise, but the donkey would not listen and was annoyed with the fox. The fox walked away silently.

As the fox hid himself in the nearby bushes, the donkey threw up his head and sang his song ...

Hearing the donkey bray, the farmer's servant rushed out with a stick, beat the donkey severely and chased him away.

Moral: Advice when most needed is least heeded.

THE FOUR LEARNED BRAHMINS

Knowledge is power. Use it wisely. Never use your powers vainly.

Once four young Brahmins were disciples of a learned guru. They spent years learning all the scriptures. And then one day, they were ready to leave their teacher's hermitage.

The four young Brahmins were excited that they had completed their learning. They were eager to test their skills. As they were going through the forest they saw the bones of a lion lying on the forest floor.

The four young Brahmins agreed to test their learning. The first Brahmin decided to put the bones together and recreate the skeleton of a lion.

The second young Brahmin, eager to
test his learning decided to give the
skeleton flesh and skin. As the others
watched he created a perfect life-like
lion.

The third young Brahmin was the cleverest of them all. He decided to try and breathe life into the body of the lion.

But the fourth Brahmin who was not as clever as the others, felt that they were using their powers in vain. When the others would not listen to him he climbed onto the branch of a tree before his friend gave life to the lion.

The fourth Brahmin watched from the tree as his friend uttered spells and sprinkled water on the lion. As soon as life entered in its body, the lion sprang up and killed the three young Brahmins.

The fourth Brahmin was horrified and filled with sorrow. His three friends would have done so well in life if only they had learnt to act wisely and not just cleverly.

Moral: Wisdom consists in knowing what to do with what you know.

THE FAITHFUL MONGOOSE

Let us take care of this poor mongoose.

One day a Brahmin saw a baby mongoose lying next to its dead mother. It was crying. The Brahmin took pity on the poor creature and took it home to his wife, who accepted to take care of it along with her baby boy.

The little mongoose and the Brahmin's son grew up like brothers. As the days passed, the little mongoose grew up fast. He now had sharp teeth and claws. As the Brahmin's wife saw the mongoose playing with her little son, she wondered...

One afternoon, when her husband was away, the Brahmin's wife had to go and fetch water. She looked around the room. Both the mongoose and her son were fast asleep. She decided to hurry back with the water.

A short while after the Brahmin's wife had left, the little mongoose suddenly jumped up from his sleep. There in front of him was a huge cobra. The brave little mongoose fought a hard battle with the snake and at last managed to kill him.

Just then the little mongoose heard the Brahmin's wife returning. He rushed to tell her how he saved his brother. But when she saw the blood, she thought that the little mongoose had killed her son. In grief- stricken rage she threw the pot on him, killing him instantly.

The Brahmin's wife rushed into her house, only to see her little son fast asleep, unharmed. On the floor a huge cobra lay dead. In a moment she realised her folly. She wept bitterly that she had killed a faithful little creature who had risked his life to save her son.

Moral: Do not judge always by appearance.

THE FOOLISH MONKEY

A group of monkeys once lived in a forest at the edge of a village. Their leader was an old and very wise monkey. All the other monkeys respected and obeyed him.

One day the villagers decided to build a temple at the outskirts of their village. The monkeys saw them at work. But they obeyed their leader and kept away.

After a whole day's work, the villagers left their tools and building material at the site and went home for a good night's rest.

Two young monkeys who were very curious started playing at the temple site when they saw that the villagers had left.

An older monkey saw the young
monkeys and called out to them in
alarm.

One of the young monkeys obeyed and went back. But the other continued to play at the site. He ignored all the others who kept calling him back.

Then the young monkey climbed on to a huge log of wood. The villagers had sawn half of it. To keep it from closing together, they had pushed a little wedge in between.

The foolish monkey got in-between the sawn log and pulled at the wedge. Suddenly, the wedge came off and the huge log snapped together crushing the poor little monkey to death.

Moral: The reward of disobedience is grief.

THE LION AND THE WOODCUTTER

There was once a lion, who lived in a jungle. He was always followed by a jackal and a crow. They ate the remains of the lion's meal.

A woodcutter used to come to the same jungle to cut wood. He lived in a small village at the edge of the jungle.

One day while the woodcutter was cuttlng wood, the lion came up behind him. The woodcutter was afraid but he did not show his fear.

The lion was surprised at the
woodcutter's invitation. He decided
to taste the woodcutter's food. The
crow and the jackal were not with the
lion that day. He liked the food very
much.

The crow and the jackal were surprised that the lion had stopped hunting. They could eat only if the lion caught a prey.

So one day they followed the lion as he went to meet the woodcutter. There they saw the lion share the woodcutter's meal. They decided to break the friendship with the woodcutter.

The next day the jackal and the crow went to the lion and pleaded with him to take them along when he went to meet his new friend. The lion agreed.

When the woodcutter saw the lion approaching him with the jackal and the crow, he quickly climbed up a tree and refused to come down.

Moral: It is easier to make friends than to keep them.

THE CROW AND THE POT OF WATER

It was a hot summers day and a poor crow was very thirsty. She flew about the forest searching for a pond or spring to drink water. But it had not rained for many days and she could not find any water.

At last she came to a village at the outskirts of the forest. To her delight she saw a pot in the backyard of a house. There was some water in the pot.

The crow flew down and perched on the mouth of the pot and dipped her beak inside to drink the water. But the water was at the bottom of the big pot. The poor crow could not reach it.

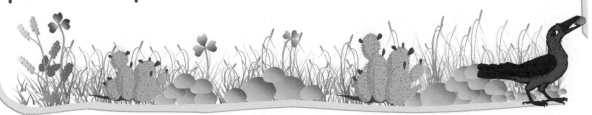

The crow was a very clever bird. She hopped down from the pot and looked around, trying to find a way to reach the water. Then she saw that there were many pebbles on the ground. Suddenly, she had an idea.

The clever crow picked one pebble after another and dropped it into the pot. After a while she could see the water slowly rising in the pot. She was very happy that her plan was working.

Soon the water had risen to the top and came up to the brim of the pot. Now the thirsty crow could drink water to her heart's content. Thus the crow by using her intelligence overcame the difficulty.

Moral: Presence of mind can be your best friend.

SHAKESPEARE
Illustrated Stories for Children

ISBN 81 7963 019-6　　Hard Cover 248 Pages　　Colour Illustration　　MRP. : 325/-

Best Selling Titles

ISBN 81 7963 007-2   54 Pages

ISBN 81 7963 008-0   66 Pages

ISBN 81 7963 009-9   68 Pages

ISBN 81 7963 010-2   62 Pages